Especially
for Raphael,
curator of the
greatest known
with love from a
author
in your
private collection!

'96

FOR THE
SAKE
OF A
CAKE

BY JOSEPHINE NOBISSO AND ANTON C. KRAJNC

RIZZOLI
NEW YORK

Koala and Alligator lay in bed.

"Go check the cake," Koala said.

"I cannot move!" Alligator replied.

"I worked so hard I almost died!"

"Get up before the cake gets burned!

And if it does, the lesson's learned

That **someone's** lazy, mean, and sly!

Now *there's* a fact you can't deny!"

Alligator got so mad

He couldn't speak. He grabbed a pad.

"I WILL NOT GO!" his note proclaimed.

Koala, bolting up, exclaimed,

"It's your turn now, so don't you shirk!

You promised me we'd share the work!"

"But who cooked our dinner, washed our dishes?"

"And who fed our dogs, baboons, and fishes?"

"**Someone** here—a slothful pest—

Should let me have some peace and rest!"

Alligator turned away

As Koala thought up mean things to say.

For a long while the room was still,

Each one claiming the stronger will.

Could a compromise be arranged?

Think quick!

Something about the air has changed!

Alligator twitched his nose.

Koala sniffed through all the bedclothes.

"What is that?" Koala yelled

'Bout something dreadful they both smelled.

"Do you think that it could be . . . ?"

"Get out from under the bed and see!"

Alligator almost spoke,

But his voice had choked up with smoke.

Koala coughed and coughed again;

No arguments from him since then.

The rumor spread both far and wide:

Koala and Alligator almost died

All because of one mistake—

Neither got up to check the cake.

Viennese Marble Guglhupf (Cake)

½ cup (4 oz.) unsalted butter
¾ cup sugar (6 oz.)
4 eggs
I tsp. vanilla extract
rind of I lemon, grated
2½ cups sifted flour
2½ tsp. baking powder
I pinch salt
6 Tbs. light cream or milk
3 oz. slivered almonds
3 oz. grated dark chocolate (bittersweet)
2 oz. sliced almonds
powdered sugar

Cream butter and sugar until fluffy. Beat in eggs, one at a time. Add vanilla extract and grated lemon rind. Beat. In another bowl, sift flour, baking powder, and salt. Fold these dry ingredients into the egg and sugar mixture, alternating with spoonfuls of light cream or milk. Divide batter into two bowls.

Add slivered almonds to one bowl of batter; mix well. Add grated chocolate to the other bowl and mix. If the batter is too firm, add a little cream or milk (batter should be thick and smooth—not sticky or too thin.)

Butter a fluted guglhupf pan (or a fluted tube pan) and sprinkle it with sliced almonds, pressing them into the flutes.

Pour half the almond batter into the pan, then add all the chocolaty batter. Add a final layer of almond batter and smooth the top with a spatula. Bake for about one hour in an oven preheated to 350°. Allow the cake to cool. Then carefully remove it from the pan and dust it with powdered sugar.

Enjoy!

First published in the United States of America in 1993
by Rizzoli International Publications, Inc.
300 Park Avenue South, New York, New York 10010

Text copyright © 1993 by Josephine Nobisso
Art copyright © 1993 by Anton C. Krajnc

Cataloging-in-Publication Data for this book
is available from the Library of Congress

Designer: Barbara Balch
Editor: Kimberly Harbour

Printed in Singapore

This one's for Victor,
For the sake of
Our Lady, Queen of Peace
—JN

To the memory of
Helmut, Gertrud, and Doris
—AK